This edition is published by special arrangement with Lothrop,
Lee & Shepard, a division of William Morrow, Publishers, Inc.

Grateful acknowledgment is made to Lothrop, Lee & Shepard
Books, a division of William Morrow & Company, Inc. for
permission to reprint *Eat Up, Gemma* by Sarah Hayes, illustrated
by Jan Ormerod. Text copyright © 1988 by Sarah Hayes;
illustrations copyright © 1988 by Jan Ormerod.

Printed in the United States of America

ISBN 0-15-300315-4

5 6 7 8 9 10   059   96   95   94

EAT UP,
GEMMA

Written by
Sarah Hayes

Illustrated by
Jan Ormerod

HARCOURT BRACE & COMPANY
Orlando Atlanta Austin Boston San Francisco Chicago Dallas New York
Toronto London

One morning we woke up late.
I couldn't find my shoes
and Gemma wouldn't eat her breakfast.
"Eat up, Gemma," said Mom,
but Gemma threw her breakfast on the floor.

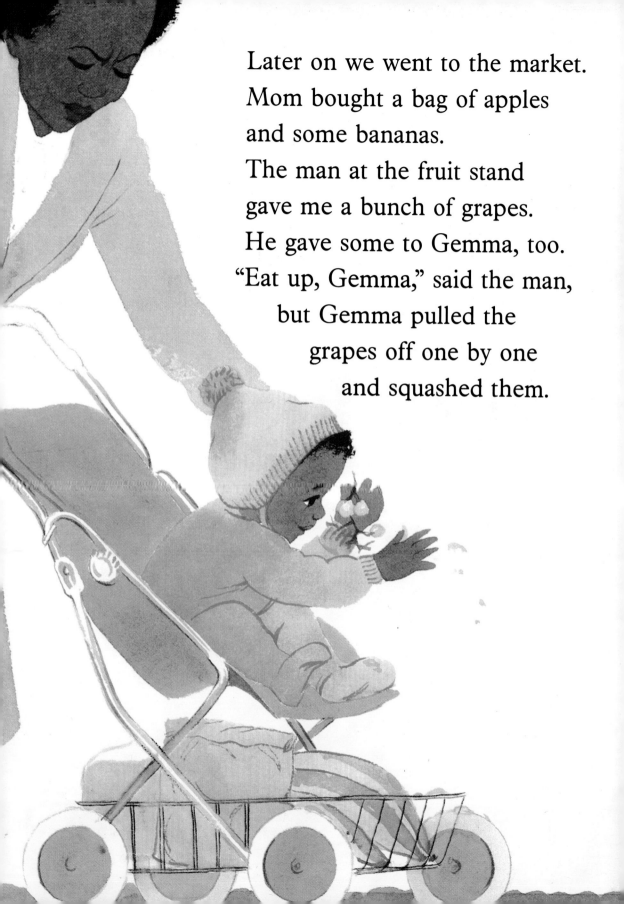

Later on we went to the market.
Mom bought a bag of apples
and some bananas.
The man at the fruit stand
gave me a bunch of grapes.
He gave some to Gemma, too.
"Eat up, Gemma," said the man,
but Gemma pulled the
grapes off one by one
and squashed them.

When we got home
Grandma had made dinner.
"Nice and spicy," Dad said,
"just how I like it."
It was nice and spicy all right.
I drank three glasses of water.
"Eat up, Gemma," said Grandma.
Gemma banged her spoon on the table
and shouted.
But she didn't eat a thing.

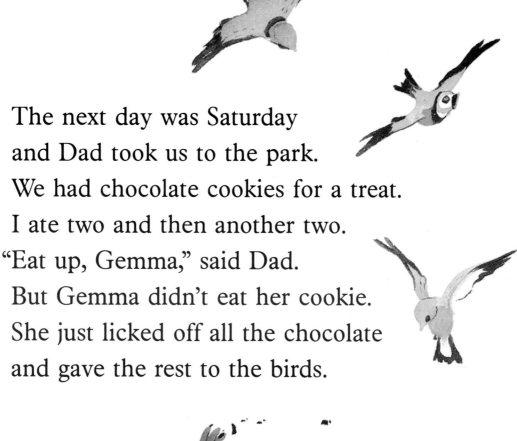

The next day was Saturday
and Dad took us to the park.
We had chocolate cookies for a treat.
I ate two and then another two.
"Eat up, Gemma," said Dad.
But Gemma didn't eat her cookie.
She just licked off all the chocolate
and gave the rest to the birds.

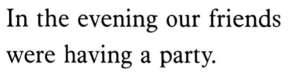
In the evening our friends
were having a party.
"Eat up, everyone," said our friends.
And we did, all except Gemma.
She sat on Grandma's knee
and gave her dinner to the dog
when Grandma wasn't looking.

After the party my friend came to stay
and we had a midnight feast.
Gemma didn't have any.
She was too tired.

In the morning we made Gemma a feast.
"Eat up, Gemma," said my friend.
Gemma picked up her toy hammer
and banged her feast to pieces.
My friend thought it was funny,
but Mom and Dad didn't.

Soon it was time for us to put on
our best clothes and go to church.
I sang very loudly.

The lady in front of us
had a hat with fruit on it.
I could see Gemma looking and looking.

When everyone was really quiet
Gemma leaned forward.
"Eat up, Gemma," she said.

Then she tried to pull
a grape off the lady's hat.
She pulled and pulled
and the lady's hat fell off.
Gemma hid her face in Dad's coat.

When we got home I had an idea.
I found a plate and a bowl.
I turned the bowl upside down
and put it on the plate.
Then I took a bunch of grapes
and two bananas and put them on the plate.
It looked just like the lady's hat.

"Eat up, Gemma," I said.
And she did.
She ate all the grapes
and the bananas.
She even tried to
eat the skins.

"Thank goodness for that," said Mom.
"We were getting worried," said Dad.
Grandma smiled at me.
I felt very proud.
"Gemma eat up," said Gemma,
and we all laughed.